D1383340

Howard Norman

WHO-PADDLED-
BACKWARD-
WITH-TROUT

art by Ed Young

Joy Street Books   Little, Brown and Company   Boston   Toronto

15318053   11113

For Keiko and Jesse — H.N.

To the Bakers, my first and finest American family,
without whom my life would not be the same — E.Y.

Text copyright © 1987 by Howard Norman
Illustrations copyright © 1987 by Ed Young

All rights reserved. No part of this book may be reproduced
in any form or by any electronic or mechanical means,
including information storage and retrieval systems,
without permission in writing from the publisher, except
by a reviewer who may quote brief passages in a review.

First Edition

Library of Congress Cataloging-in-Publication Data

Norman, Howard A.
Who-Paddled-Backward-with-Trout.

Summary: A young Cree Indian boy, Trout-with-
Flattened-Nose, is not fond of his given name and
seeks to earn a new one that is more flattering.
1. Cree Indians — Legends. 2. Indians of North
America — Canada — Legends. [1. Cree Indians — Legends.
2. Indians of North America — Canada — Legends.
3. Names, Personal — Folklore]   I. Young, Ed, ill.
II. Title.
E99.C88N67   1987   398.2′08997   [E]   87-2725
ISBN 0-316-61182-4

WOR

Published simultaneously in Canada
by Little, Brown & Company (Canada) Limited
PRINTED IN THE UNITED STATES OF AMERICA

*T*his story was told to me by George Wesukmin
("Sour Berry") when he was eighty-two years old. He lived
in a Cree Indian village near Gods Lake in northern
Manitoba, Canada. In his village, if you were
not happy with the name your parents chose for
you, you could try to earn a new name.

In one Cree village lived a boy who kept
bumping into things. Once he walked right
into the side of a hut. Another time he wandered
into a tree. Each thing he bumped into
flattened his nose a little more.

One day an old man in the village told the boy's parents about a dream. "In my dream," he said, "a clumsy trout kept bumping into things. The trout bumped into rocks and logs. He even bumped into my canoe!"

"That sounds just like our son!" the boy's mother said. "Old man, may we name him after your dream?" — because so far the parents had been unable to find a proper name for their son.

"You may," the old man said, and so the young boy became known as Trout-with-Flattened-Nose.

As the boy grew older, he became more and more unhappy with his name. "I want a name I can be proud of," he told his parents.

He ran from his village. "I'll be back when
I've thought of a new name for myself!"

When he had run a long way, the boy sat down under a tree. He thought hard. The first name he came up with was Who-Can-Sneak-Up-on-Owls. "Yes, that is a fitting name for me!" he decided. "If I can sneak up on owls, who can hear even a mouse scampering over wet leaves, then I can sneak up on any animal!"

He started home, pleased with himself for having come up with such a good idea so quickly. Along the way, he happened upon a tree full of sleeping owls. "Here's a chance to try out my new name," he whispered to himself. He crouched down and began to creep toward the tree.

Suddenly he sneezed. "A-choo! A-choo! A-choo!"

Each sneeze woke up an owl.

"Hey! What's all the noise? We can't sleep," one called down.

But when the boy tried to answer, he just sneezed some more. "A-choo! A-choo! A-choo!"

"Let's get out of here," another owl said. "It's too noisy!"

Before the boy could stop sneezing, the owls all flew away.

The boy sat down under the empty owl tree and said, "Maybe that was not quite the right name for me." He thought some more.

"I've got it!" he cried. "I'll be named Who-Can-Echo-Better-Than-a-Loon. That way I'll have a strong voice that can carry across any lake. I'll have the biggest voice around. Everyone will hear me!"

He hurried back toward his village to tell his parents.

Along the way, he came upon a lake. He climbed onto a boulder, drew in a deep breath, and shouted, "I'm here! I'm here! I'm here!"

He cupped his ears and listened to the lake, but he heard nothing.

He tried a little louder. "Hello! It's me! I'm here!"

Still the lake was perfectly quiet.

Suddenly a loon flew past him and dove into the lake.

"No doubt that loon has been catching my echoes in midair and swallowing them!" the boy grumbled.

At that, the loon flew straight up out of the water and called, "Yes! It's *my* echoing lake!"

The loon's words could be heard over and over again. "It's *my* echoing lake! It's *my* echoing lake! It's *my* echoing lake!"

The boy kicked a few rocks into the lake, but even the rocks were silent.

He sat down against the boulder and once again asked himself, "What should my new name be?" And he thought of what he most liked to do in the world — paddle a canoe!

He ran back to his parents' house. "My new name is Who-Paddles-a-Canoe-Better-Than-Anyone," he announced proudly.

"That's not the way of our village," his father said. "You can't just have whichever name you want. You have to *earn* a new name!"

"You must also ask permission of the old man who first gave you your name. He has since become a trout," his mother said. "Go paddle out and find him."

"How will I know which trout he is?" asked the boy.

"Paddle to the middle of the lake," his father said. "Wait there until a trout bumps into your paddle. That will be the trout you are searching for. Once he has knocked himself out against your paddle, lift him into the canoe. When he wakes up, ask permission to change your name.

"And don't forget to take along a spare paddle," his father added.

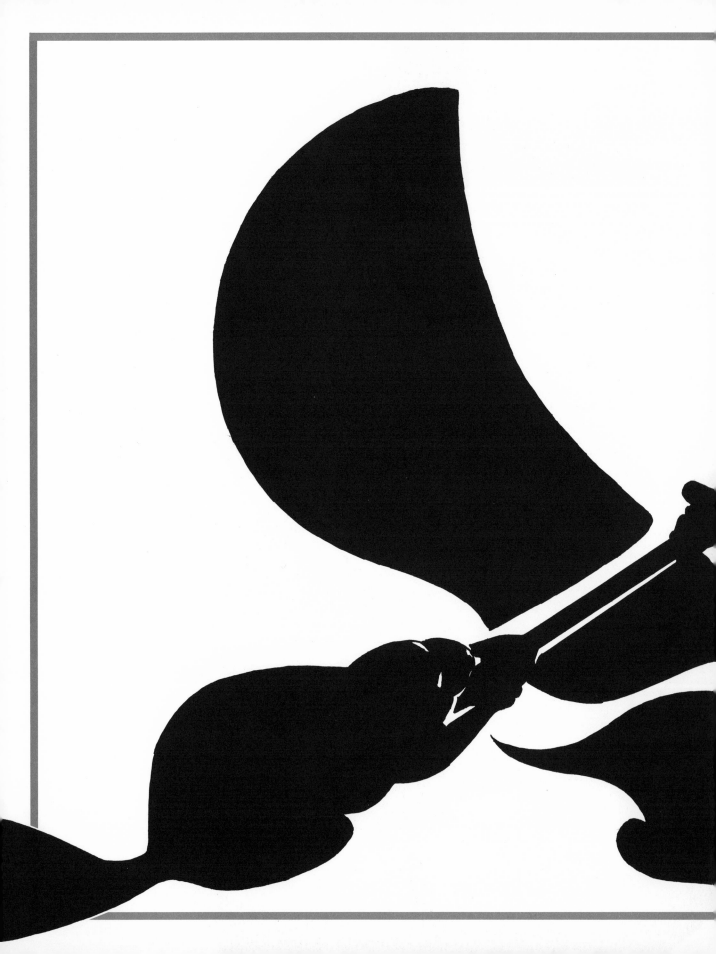

The boy happily began to paddle out on the lake. "Soon I'll earn the perfect name for myself!" he said. "Who-Paddles-a-Canoe-Better-Than-Anyone!" But as he dipped his paddle into the lake, it became so heavy that he could barely move it. It took all his strength to lift the paddle from the water. When he finally did, he saw why: a beaver had chomped right onto it!

"Give me this paddle!" the beaver demanded. "It comes from an old tree I gnawed down a long time ago."

"No, it's *my* paddle," the boy said. "I need it to get my new name." Holding tight, he raised the paddle high and flung the beaver back into the lake.

He looked at the paddle. It was badly chewed up. "I can't use this!" he said. "But that won't stop me. I have a spare paddle!"

But when he searched for the other paddle, it was nowhere to be found.

A second beaver was swimming away with it!

Using the chewed-up paddle, the boy began
to chase the thief, but in all the excitement he
forgot to paddle on both sides. The canoe began
to spin in a circle, faster and faster, until the
boy was so dizzy that he fell into the water.
Splash! By the time he managed to climb back
into the canoe, he was worn out.

"Lucky for me the sun is so bright today," he
said. "It will dry me out."

He lay down in the canoe and fell fast asleep.

When he woke up, he was floating in the middle of the lake. "Oh, well, now that I'm here," he told himself, "I can look for that clumsy trout!"

He dangled the chewed-up paddle in the water, hoping the trout would bump into it.

As he waited he decided to fish. Right away he felt a tug. He pulled and pulled — it was the missing paddle! The beavers had chewed it into the shape of a big trout!

"This isn't the trout I'm looking for," the boy muttered.

Just then the paddle said, "You're right, I'm not!" It leaped off the fishing line and swam away.

When the boy looked over to shore, he saw
the beavers huddled together, laughing at him.

"One paddle is chewed up, another is in the
shape of a trout," he said. "But those beavers
won't stop me!"

He began to fish again. Soon he had another
trout on the end of his line. It dove deep and
began to rise again, right up against the bottom
of the canoe. Thump, thump, again and again!

"You must be the trout I'm looking for!" the
boy shouted.

He pulled the clumsy trout into the canoe,
then ran his fingers along its sides to make sure
this fish wasn't made of wood.

"I need your permission to change my name
to Who-Paddles-a-Canoe-Better-Than-Anyone,"
he demanded.

The trout looked him over carefully. "So
that's the name you've decided on, eh?
Hmmm. . . . First I must see you do some
paddling."

"But I have only this chewed-up paddle left,"
the boy protested.

"Actually, you have *no* paddles left," the
trout observed. "Look!"

On shore the beavers were inspecting the
chewed-up paddle. The beaver-thief had stolen
it, too, while the boy was talking to the trout.

"What will I do now?" the boy cried.

"Don't worry," the trout said. "I'll tow you."

The boy tied a rope to the trout's tail and tossed him in the water. But, the clumsy trout began pulling the canoe right toward the sharp rocks near shore.

"Trout, stay away from those rocks!" the boy shouted. "Look out!" But the trout was under water and couldn't hear him.

He had to do something quickly. Reaching into the water, he grabbed the fish, and using the trout as a paddle, he paddled backward as fast as he could. The canoe veered away just in time.

The boy paddled to a calm shallow, pulled the canoe ashore, tossed the trout into the water, and sat down to rest. "Phew!" he exclaimed.

The trout stuck his face out of the water. "*Now* I'm ready to give you a new name," he declared. "You have paddled like no one I have ever seen!"

The boy began to smile.

He strode to the edge of the lake and he held his arms out wide. "I wish everyone in the village could have seen me: Who-Paddles-a-Canoe-Better-Than-Anyone!"

"Wait a moment," the trout said slowly. "I said you paddled like no one I have ever seen. So I am giving you the name Who-Paddled-Backward-with-Trout."

The boy could hardly speak. "But I thought . . . ! I wanted . . ."

"It's a fine, strong name," the trout interrupted. "And you most certainly have earned it!"